HODDER CHILDREN'S BOOKS

First published in Great Britain in 2011
by Hodder and Stoughton

This paperback edition published in 2017

A CIP catalogue record for this book
is available from the British Library.

ISBN: 978 1 444 94902 5

10 9 8 7 6 5 4 3 2 1

Printed and bound in China

Hodder Children's Books
An imprint of Hachette Children's Group
Part of Hodder and Stoughton
Carmelite House
50 Victoria Embankment
London EC4Y 0DZ
An Hachette UK Company

www.hachette.co.uk
www.hachettechildrens.co.uk

FOR MUM

MONIKA AND LUKA...
DON'T WORRY, BE HAPPY!

www.davidmelling.co.uk

www.huglessdouglas.co.uk

Don't Worry, Hugless Douglas

David Melling

Hodder Children's Books

Douglas and his dad were playing.
'What's behind your back?' asked Douglas.
'Not that hand, the other one.'
Dad smiled,
'Something for you!'

It was a new woolly hat.

'Wow!' said Douglas.
'Thanks, Dad.'
Douglas had never
had a woolly
hat before.
He couldn't wait
to show his friends.

'Look after it,'
said Dad.

But Douglas was
already off!

'Look at me!' shouted Douglas.

'Snazzy hat, Douglas!' baaed the sheep.

'I can even do cartwheels in it!' he whooped.
And he did. Again. And again.

Until something didn't feel right.

Douglas gasped. His new woolly hat had turned into one long string of spaghetti!

'That's not supposed to happen,' he gulped.
'Don't worry, Douglas,' said the sheep.
'We'll fix it.'
They wound it into a ball and squished it
back into shape.

'Any good?' they asked.
'**NO!**' said Douglas.

'Cow is a good
thinker,' said
the sheep.
'She'll know
what to do.'

Cow thought she had a very good idea.
'Pretty!' she said.

'**NO**,' said Douglas.

'Don't worry, Douglas!' chirped a swoopy bird,
'I can use this for my nest.'

'NO, YOU CAN'T,'
yelped Douglas.
'That's my new woolly hat!'

'Doesn't look like a woolly hat,'
said the swoopy bird.
'Anyway,' he puffed,
'it doesn't fit.'
And he dropped it out of the tree.

Just then it began to rain.

Douglas was really
worried now.
'What's my dad going
to say?' he mumbled.

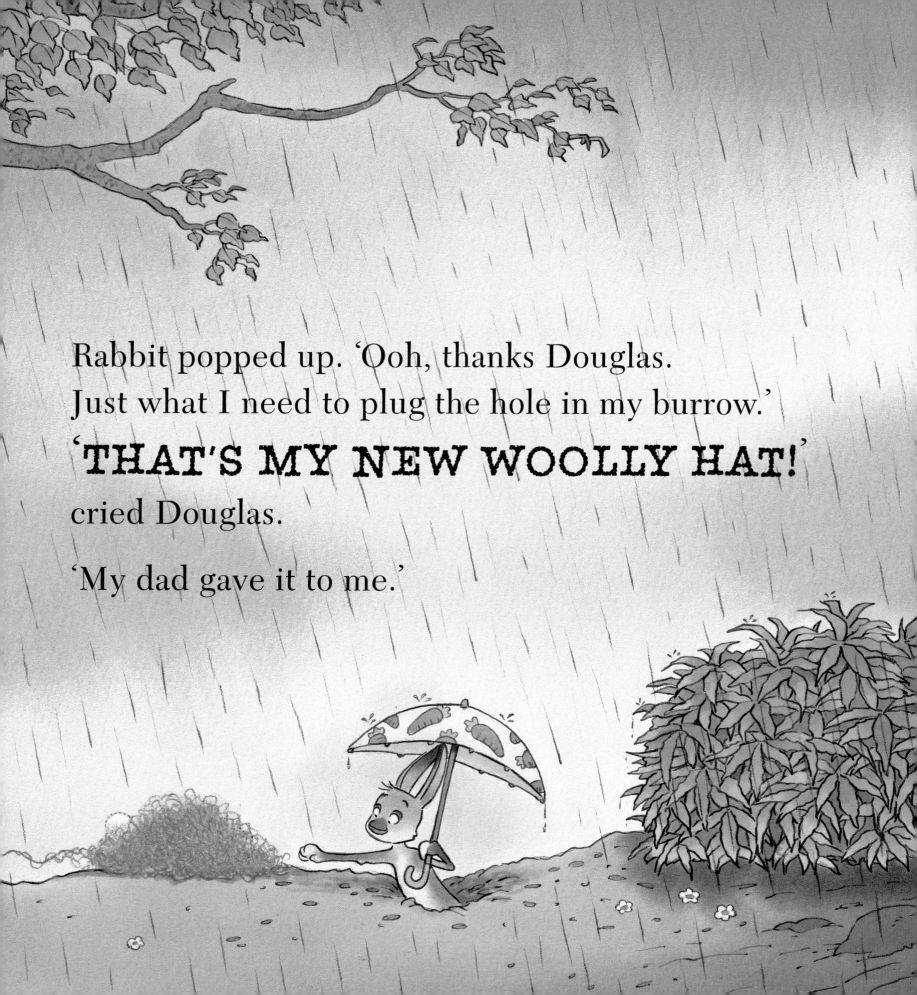

Rabbit popped up. 'Ooh, thanks Douglas.
Just what I need to plug the hole in my burrow.'

'**THAT'S MY NEW WOOLLY HAT!**'

cried Douglas.

'My dad gave it to me.'

'Sorry,' said Rabbit, 'I didn't know.
Come here,' she said and wiped his nose.

'What am I going to do?' sniffed Douglas.

Rabbit looked thoughtful.

'Why don't you just tell your dad what happened?
He's nice, your dad, he'll understand.'

Maybe Rabbit was right. Douglas picked up his wet spaghetti hat and trudged back home.

'Oh, Douglas,' sighed his mum.
'Look at you!'

'Where's your new hat?'
asked his dad.

Douglas told them
everything.

'Don't worry, Douglas,' said Dad.
'I've got something for you.
Guess which hand?'
Douglas wasn't sure.
'Here's **my** hat,' laughed Dad.

'You'll soon grow into it!'

Banana Hat

Nappy Hat

I Don't Like Peas Hat

Follow-The-Leader Hat

Spot-The-Difference Hat

Best Friends Hat

Pants Hat

Peek-a-Boo Hat

Wig Hat

Weather Hat

Love Hat

Potty Hat

Family Hat

WORRY TREE

Douglas is really worried when his hat unravels, but he feels much better when he tells his mum and dad. This tree is so big and strong it can hold all your worries for you. Why not draw your own Worry Tree? Now write down your worries, big and small, and stick them along the branches. Sharing worries can help make them less scary. Take a sticker away when something doesn't worry you anymore.